MW01699888

Fair Fun

By Kelly Kirstein

Illustrated by Metaxa Cunningham

Happy ... Noo!! Grandma & Grandpa Can't wait for you to read us this book all our love Forever & always!

For Kelly

Aethereal Publishing
ISBN-13: 978-0986568077
ISBN-10: 0986568074

A day at the fair is huge fun for me.
There is oodles to do, plenty to see.

First a parade with batons and cartwheels,
Marching bands, big floats, old automobiles.

With the parade now over let the carnival begin!
The rides! The food! All of the prizes to win!
The pretty pink pony on the Merry-Go-Round
Makes me dizzy when my feet touch the ground!

I throw the darts to burst all the balloons.
I win a stuffed bear and it's still only noon!
I spot the Candied Apple I really must eat,
A sweet and delightful, delicious treat!

POP THE
BALLOONS

Next I become a tiger when they paint my face,
Then I join my dad in a three-legged race.
I order myself a large ice cream cone,
Three scoops of chocolate to eat on my own.

FINISH

Then I feed the bunnies at the petting zoo,
And the pigs and ducks and the donkeys, too!

21

The One Man Band makes me clap and sing,
As his contraption makes clings, dings and pings.

The striker shows everyone if you are strong,
With flashing lights, bells and gong!
I pick up the hammer making a mighty swing,
The crowd lets a cheer when I make the bells ring.

In the Haunted House I let out a scream,
Then I order myself one more ice cream.

HAHA
BOO

The man on stilts is so wobbly and tall,
I hold my breath, I am scared he will fall.

At the Fun House Mirrors I can't wait to see,
The wide, and the small, and the really tall me.
I ride the slide fast ALL the way down,
Just in time to hug the big, funny clown.

FUN HOUSE

The Dragon Coaster goes fast and high,
It twists and turns me towards the sky.

Next thing I know I feel sick to my tummy,
I run rather quickly to go tell my mommy!
I tell her about all the food I have tried:
"Cotton Candy, Popcorn, Elephant Ears, French Fries,
Mini-Donuts, Corn-Dogs, and ONLY one Milkshake!"
She said, "Well, that would explain your stomach ache!"

FRANK'S PIZZA
SAM'S ICE CREAM
POP!
ZZZ

On the Ferris-Wheel things are small below,
I see the fair grounds and all their side shows.
My sister grabs me when we reach the top.
My brother yells, "Faster!" As she screams, "Stop!"

Then the magician saws his assistant in two.
How he did it? I have no clue.
Then he covers her up with his big, black cloak,
And she's back together with a Poof of Smoke!

I race to the Dunk-Tank with a mad dash,
To throw my ball hard and wait for a splash.
The man in the swimsuit gives me a grin.
Then looks rather shocked when I make him fall in.

I drive my Bumper Car into the others,
Especially my mom's, dad's, sister's and brother's.

To top it all off and to end my day,
I sit on Dad's shoulders at the fireworks display.
The fair is now closing and the end is near
But I'm not sad. They'll be back next year!

The End

With Love From:

Lenord, Delyn & Floyd Kirstein
Jackie and Wyatt Janes
Lois Rollier
Sheryl & Ron Cossette
Amanda Pylypow
Ethan & Meagan Pylypow
Sonja Haywood
Ruth & Gary Ogilvie
Larry & Brenda Murphy
Lori & Corie Cooper
Stuart & Tammy Burke
Marlene & John Rollier
Corey & Terry Vanderploeg
Carter Tomczak
Brett & Joelene Letendre
Tracey Schockenmaier
Laurie French
Carolyn Swart Dressler
Keith, Vera and Kelly McLeod
Kirby & Jane Muyres
Shelli Orava
Cliff & Donna Galey

Jason & Kristal Galey
Maja Wynes
Todd & Pat Quinlan
Jody Rollier-Young
Nikkita Cossette
Leo & Geane Quinlan
Charlene Goddard
Shirley Anger
Dorothy & Marlon Kirstein
Jill & Keiron Klevyer
Crystal & Tom Hall
Jaclynn Quinlan
Melanie Ross Nielsen
Andrea Murrant
Kelvin McElderry
Marina Coldwell
Wayne& Tammy Cote
Wanda & Allan Sunde
Brian & Karen Froehler
Donna & James Rollier
Alice Green
Coralie Koples
Joan & Jimmy Smith
Zach & Ryan Belitsky

Sandra Herman
Barb Pinder
Sheila Oja
Shirley Szoke
Audrey Gaetz
Linda & Rich Plouffe
Sunni & Chris Paszcza
Lora Stenberg
Jason Stenberg
Gordon & Laurel Koples
Judy Andreson
S/T Gagnon
Carol Keeley
Andrew Gaetz
Lynn Dressler
Ken Stenberg
Karen Medin
Jason Stenberg
Kristin McKenzie
Randy and Lana McKenzie
Ken and Carole Johnston
Metaxa Cunningham
...and Danielle Lee

47854347R00025

Made in the USA
Charleston, SC
19 October 2015